The Night

Stalker

Written by:

J.E. Shook

Dedication

I dedicate this novel to Ashley for her continued support, love, and for always pushing me towards my goals.

Contents

Acknowledgments

I want to acknowledge all the people who have Dyslexia and ADHD and for the underdogs.

I believe that if you work hard enough, you can achieve anything in life.

Chapter 1

Far below the cliff, the hungry sea gnawed at its ankle. Someone once said that paradise is to be found where seagulls soar beneath your feet. They were arcing and spinning between the moonshine's spells. A haunting and resonant cry would occasionally reverberate from the cliffs. The vast sight stretching to the horizon was breathtaking. The Prussian-blue velvet vault above seemed to solder into the liquid silver blanket underneath. A lone cormorant sped out to sea, sleek wings fluttering, to the point where water and sky merged and vanished from view.

The sea's slurpy slapping sounded muffled, like a metronomic hum. In their liquid robes, the waves were just napping, languid, and slumbering. They dribbled up to the secluded cove's beach, then shivered and dripped their sea spray across its surface, whisking the stones before releasing them. A frigid electrical current flowed across the air. We were shivering. The wind was howling. The sea was simmering.

Its vast guts shook, a rumbling from the depths, bloated to its constricted depths. The sea hissed, cleansed, polished, and lashed the pebbles before splashing back, causing stone dashed sand to teem. It hissed, slid, dashed the sand, and let go; fizzed, spit, and seethed the beach, and let go; sizzled, slapped, and swished the stones, and let go.

The mesmeric beauty of its beat was one to make the heart throb. It was one to make those around it realize that the sea was its own master, the artist, the king, torching its own symphony. And the song was not done yet. The wind, the sea's midwife, served another lord and whipped it into a frenzy.

Just then, the echo of a raspy rumbling from the enraged sea came to those who dared to stand there, a tremulousness to fear. The waves were slobbering, slurping, and slurping with their salty lips. They slammed into the sheltering cove's cliff, then hesitated and lunged with malice onto its ankle, driving it against the rock before releasing. A rumor of its malevolence passed across the too-proud shores.

The moon shook, curling up like gentle fire. The oceans had glazed, and the waves had buzzed, being carried away by the gasping sounds of winds. The beams of moonlight forayed against the waves that splashed. But just then, a little while later, the wind came to die down. The sea bubbled, trembling, throbbing to its rotten beat; its malicious soul stirred, a warning from the ages. Suddenly, rip-tide rolls heaved as the sea foamed, crashed, pounded, and bashed the cliff-foot before sloshing back. It foamed and frothed, plunged down hard, and pummeled the hated cliffs; it lathered and lacerated, bucked waves and buckled itself; it smacked and smashed, surging waves and expunging its awful rage. Its hissy fit over, it swelled once more, juddered, and was still.

Right in the midst of the Carpathian mountains ranges, connecting the seas, there stood a village too proudly not much far from the shore.

In the distance, the serrated mountains loomed. The people in the tent could see through the dark; the moonlight had helped, and the voices from the woods seemed quite sinister. The mountains were flour-white and loomed over the landscape. As their sight paved the way, they could see a snow chute separate itself and trundle down one of the hills. It fell over the tangled edge and plunged into the pit below. The silence that crept shortly behind welcomed chills that ran down the spine of the woman lying in the midwife's tent. It froze our marrow to think we would be climbing in those circumstances the next day.

The mountain's heaven-touching pinnacle was bathed in bright light. In a bristling, the thin and shivering moonlight stabbed the snow. It could be thought that the heat had pushed the snow away from the hip of the time-worn mountain. The peaks of the mountains protruded like a row of thorns across the sight of nature. As time passed, the air grew arctic cold. It was the village that had been home to a few hundred people and all the rest of the concealed existence that they remained in the dark to. It was there a mother wailed in agony, the mother who had gone into labor – a warning that the heavens would cry soon enough. The delivery was, as always, grim and arduous, but she knew that it was inevitable to attain the child she had been nurturing inside her body for the past nine months. And so, she held on through the pain. She held on to the hope of life getting much more beautiful than it had heretofore ever been. She had hope, and so, she held on to it. She held on to the happiness that was about to come along with the child. And so, she waited. She waited for the moment when she was going to hold her child in her hands for the first time ever. The weather was cold, and she shivered. But at that time, she was quite unsure if it was the wintriness weather that had her trembling, shaking. Or was it the fact that she did not know what future and fate had in store for her? She remained clueless, not too eager to find out, for she had a feeling that it was about to be bad… whatever it was.

She was there, screaming in pain, vacillating in agony, fading away with the uncertainty of the future with each passing second. Her loving husband had held her hand through it, looking her in the eyes, telling her that it was going to be alright. The midwife screamed, "Push," quite a few times from under the cloth that was there to cover the lower body of the mother.

What could it be that made her quake and tremor as she thought about it? What would make her whole body shake at the thought of it, if not the pain that came with the delivery? She was not sure, but she continued to feel how fearful she was. Chills raced down her spine.

She had known it to be precisely what a mother does – anything for the child, everything for the child. And with a smile on her face, she kept thinking about the lengths she was willing to have gone to for her child, the boundaries she was willing to cross for the young guy. She sniveled – wiping her eyes away from the sporadic tears that tendered on her face. She screamed as her hand grasped the husband's a bit too tightly. And with the courage to do it and yet not the energy to do it, she pushed. And she kept pushing.

And there he was… so little… too little. Her child. Her beautiful child. And she did not give a thought about what the world around her meant for her, not caring about all that was written for her by her fate and the future that approached. All she cared about was the person she had just pushed out of my body, the one who had left her body, entering her heart - forever and after.

She almost passed out as the child slipped into her loving arms. The next two sentences that came out of her mouth were the souvenirs of her life changing forever. As she held the child crying child in her arms, wrapped entirely in a towel, she mouthed in a soothingly low-pitched voice to her son, "It's a boy!" She continued to whisper, not interrupting the voice of her baby crying, "I'm a mom now! Nobody's taking him away from me. Not now. Not ever." Bittersweet memories? Perhaps. Yet still, the uncertainty was at its zenith, her love still prevailing.

There he was... her Tepes – little as ever. At that moment, she knew one of the few people that her world revolved around, one of the only few people that she loved without conditions and without limits. She knew that it was the last time that she was happy to see him cry. He looked somewhat like her, perhaps much more beautiful. His features were sharp, my nose stood tall, and his eyes were big. To her, his eyes showed so much; they illustrated the determination he would grow to hold, the kind of man he would be. She knew that her son would grow into a great kid, and she knew at that moment that she was going to love her to her last breath, not knowing when that would be. It was as though it was love at first sight and before, yet one thing was for certain; it was love at its finest.

Many thoughts paraded over her head as she lay there on the hospital bed. And each of the thoughts continually reminded her of the challenges that she had yet to face once she left the midwife's tent. At that moment, she was sure that life was about to show her massive difficulties that would be necessary for raising me up, but they did not matter, for she knew that she would climb mountains for the child and that she would swim oceans just to see him happy, to see him smile. And she knew that she had her family on her side, and she knew that she had the love that it would take, and that was everything that she would ever need. At that time, she was sure that she was ready and willing to face each of them head-on.

It was the late 1400s when Tepes Tupaco was growing up in a small village in Romania, a village known to people as Bram. Growing up, he had only known his father, for he was the only one around him. Formal education from the village's school became meant to him only much as what others around him desired and aspired, yet something that he never really went for. Tepes flourished into a young man wanting more and more from his life. A mysterious man for children of his age, he would sit back at night, gazing up the mountains, replaying in his head all the fables and tales that talked about the horror that lurked in the woods.

The next day would arrive for him to be something that was long and much-awaited. His friends played in the hills of the mountains. They would play, hunt, and fish. Tepes had loved being outdoor, never really wanting to go home to the strict father and a mother who was never there.

Being in nature had him feel free, as though there was no worry in the world around them, as though there was nothing that could ever stop him from wanting what he had wanted, achieving what he had desired to be. And so, he would stay in the woods long as he could, knowing that he would eventually have to go back to his father's shop.

Mr. Mihai Tupaco, his old man, had loved him. And perhaps for that very reason, he was a detail-oriented man, always wanting what was best for his son. Or perhaps, it was because of the fact that his wife had passed on to the worlds that followed shortly. It was a fact that Tepes remained unknown to, for Mihai had thought that knowing that he killed his mother would turn out to be something that would trouble the little boy for the rest of his life. And the boy not knowing the biggest truth about his life was something that ate the father alive from the inside, a feeling that would sit at his stomach, slowly growing to the walls of his beating heart. And he would flicker his eyes, holding back his tears, knowing that it was not really his son's fault either.

But what had let him go to sleep with the arrival of the night would be the fact that his beloved wife got to hold her son. Even though it lasted no more than 20 minutes, she got to pass the smile that Mihai had never seen on her face ever before. It was the kind of smile that jolted him like an electric current of a megawatt. And his heart skipped a beat, knowing that life was beautiful in that moment. But then, like any other moment, the good one passed too, and along it took the one epic love of his life, the most beautiful amidst women. The poignant memory of the past was what had brought him pain, yet the hope of meeting her very soon, the desire of the same thing. And he would go to sleep, knowing that he would have to wake up early the next morning, or there would be people in the village walking the streets without shoes.

See, he was the only cobbler in the village, running the only shoe shop in all of Bram. Tepes had started working and learning the trade at a very young age. His father had taken him to the shop quite frequently: there was no one to look after him when his father was gone for work. His father had always thought and wanted for Tepes to grow up and take over the shop, becoming a cobbler too.

The kid was a very fast learner, a rigorous man, and a hard worker. And so, quite often, if not always, he would come to please his father. And just then, he would see the smile on his father's face, one that would let him know that there was more to it – the sadness of heartache, the loss of love, the wanting to meet someone, and the missing of a loved one.

During the summers, Tepes would roam the mountainside with his friends when he would not be working. And in the bitter-cold Romanian winters, he would stay inside with his father, who would tell the kid tales about wolves, bears, beasts, and vampires. He was not really a child to be scared through stories, and he was not one to shake and tremble at the name of a vampire. In fact, there would then be quite a few questions racing across his mind.

Vampires?

Beasts?

How much of it is true, anyway?

Are these not just some tales written to scare the kids?

Are these not just some tales to keep the children from lurking around in the woods?

How are these scary?

Time moved on as Tepes started to grow up. He was a good child, one who had ambitions and was not too scared to get to them. He became popular as he worked in the shoe shop and got to know everyone who lived in his small village. With the passage of each day, the child grew better and better at the job that his aging father expected of him. He grew to work more and more on what his father had wanted to work on, leaving no stone unturned to make him happy. Relying on his son, Mihai started to work less, trusting his son to carry the workload.

Tepes had also started to help the people around the village. He helped build homes, businesses, and buildings and maintain the Bram graveyard. The graveyard was full of the people who once resided in and loved the village. And all those who had been, they were here, in the graveyard that Tepes was working on. The boy in his late teens was working with his friends under adult supervision, proving that he would one day be a pillar of the community. He had shown determination and perseverance, a man with grit.

It was at this time he met someone. And just then, there was this feeling in his heart, one that he had never felt before. It was as though he had felt the loving embrace of a mother, the tender scolding of a father, the care of a sister, and the memories made with a brother. He felt all that at once. It was as though the world around him had stopped moving, as though he was a part of something much bigger than just himself. Her eyes had shone, and Tepes dared to stare inside as he was drawn in to see the swirling emotions at the end of them, a beautiful path to her magnificent soul.

Raina was an alluring young lady with a pixie-like nose that dropped prettily from its peak. Her eyes were like the stars – the way they drew you in to explore the swirling emotions held in their depths. The dark of her pupil was enclosed with a jag silver fire, swallowed by sapphire blue. At one glance, her eyes merely shone, but if someone ventured to look closer, they could clearly see the ultimate joy of love, the limitless hope of a bright future, and an unwavering spirit that would give up under no circumstance. The emotions held in her eyes were deep and vivid, and they said everything that she had in mind, everything that she was not really able to articulate.

The blond of her hair tousled and eventually tumbled over her shoulders – a mess of perfection. The dimples pressed against her healthy cheeks would give way to a fine smile, a smile that the world had needed. She was everything that the world required in order to carry on. Raina was the goodness that people thought to be long gone from the face of the earth.

She was a local girl, growing up without much wealth. The girls in the village would cook, wash the clothes, and do the hard labor jobs with the boys when it was needed of them. Being in her mid-teens, her father would not let her go out with a boy of her age. Her father was protective of her, knowing that the boys never really meant good intentions toward the girls.

Yet, defying her father, Raina and Tepes got to spend time together while working on different projects for the town. They ended up working a lot together in the graveyard, the one that was becoming a home to more and more people with the dusk of each sun and the dawn of each moon. Perhaps it was because of a strand sickness that was killing almost a third of the people of Europe, a sickness that no one ever really understood. Or perhaps it was because of something else, someone else – that people knew less about. But as time went on, the two of them continued to work for the town's goodness in their spare time. Though they thought of themselves to be people who knew much, they remained unaware of all the things that lurked around in the forest under the beautiful moon and shivering stars.

Chapter 2

Time goes on as it always will, and in the poor town of Bram, people grew, people aged, and people died. As Tepes and Raina grew older, they took over the cobbler shop and ran the graveyard. Then, with Raina's father's blessing, the happy couple made it official and public, doing everything as a couple, and, on a warm spring day, in front of a few family members, they got married.

As Tepes' father grew into old age, he began to grow sick and weak and finally had to retire from the shop, leaving Tepes in charge of the small shop. While running the store, travelers stopped in for repairs and told Tepes' stories of these new beasts, new monsters, new horrors popping up in Europe, and attacking people at night in their homes. They warned one another that it may one day reach Bram as more and more people travel through town, getting from one place to the next. Tepes laughed about the stories as seen then as a fairytale. When Tepes met his wife at home later that night, he told her the stories, and she did not find these stories as funny as he did.

Raina said it was God's way of punishing those who did not follow His path and lead a life of sin. Raina believed that it was a curse that was worse than death. Tepes, who treasured a happy marriage, agreed to make her happy and never thought much about it.

Even with a significant sickness covering the earth, Bram was a safe and healthy place to live. Bram was a good stop for traders, sellers, and travelers to visit and stay for the night. Times were getting better for the Tupaco family, and Tepes had a full day's work every day, and it was so much that he had to stop working at the graveyard, so Raina took over as full-time caretaker of the cemetery. Soon after, Raina had to leave her job as caretaker and tell Tepes the excellent news. She was pregnant and was going to have their first child.

Tepes was excited and did everything to make sure Raina was taken care of and that their child would have everything it would need to live a happy and healthy life. When the time came, Raina gave birth to a baby girl, whom they named Zora Tupaco. Still being poor in a small town, she had a happy childhood. A sister, little Peti Tupaco, was born only two years later. Then again, two years later, a brother, Bolek Tupaco, was born. For a time, Tepes and his family were pleased, happy, thrilled, and at peace.

As life came and went so fast in those tough times, the significant sickness was still spreading across the world and unknown to the Tupaco family and the rest of Romina. It was slowly creeping towards them, and there was no way to see it coming and no way to prepare for what it was about to do.

Chapter 3

Tepes was now with a complete family, a wife, two daughters, a son, and a store that was always full of customers. Tepes felt that he was living a good and simple life. As his kids grew, they started to excel at their studies – the girls were a little bit better than the boy, but everyone was doing well. While in school again, the kids heard stories of a magical sickness called *the black death* and of these things called *vampires*. The rumors said that they die and then undie to come back and feed on the blood of the living as a mindless beast that hunts people at night. Tepes told his kids to ignore such fairytales and stick to chores and schoolwork.

His father, now bedridden due to old age, was feeling sick and tried to get Tepes to take the stories more seriously. His father had wanted him to even prepare if they were to ever face the black death and maybe even the monsters it may bring. But being a responsible adult, he still refused to listen.

Being too busy with his work, the shop needed more help as worn-out travelers needed new shoes and repairs to old ones. With his father unable to work, his wife and kids all stepped in to pick up the slack. The kids continued to do great in school and worked hard, learning how to be cobblers in the family shop and providing all the labor and help. Tepes needed to run his business without his father.

His wife Raina was a beauty that had aged like fine wine, and his kids were intelligent, strong, and hard working. Between work in the shoe shop and going to class, the kids kept hearing the rumors, the whispers of death, and the sickness that continued to grow.

Even though this poison had been spared in Bram and they were lucky enough to avoid it, so far, fears were starting to build as it was said that the sickness and death were growing and getting worse and that soon it would take all of Europe. As the people of Bram tried to stay calm, they knew that the more travelers came and went through their small village, the greater the chances were of sickness coming to them. But with the small finally booming, they could not afford to shut the town down.

Here lay a prodigious problem for the people of Bram. Soon enough, the town's fears came true when a traveler who was staying at the local inn was spitting up blood and died of consumption.

And just then, fears and suspicions started to grow as the first signs of sickness arrived in the quiet village of Bram.

Chapter 4

While not the black death, Bram had its first taste of sickness. A stranger from another land had brought sickness into town and died. People in town now feared what was about to come their way. Within only a few weeks, one of the school kids became deadly ill, and within days, the child died. Then in the following weeks, a baker, a farmer and his family, and the mayor fell ill and died quickly. Unlike the first traveler who had spat blood, the townspeople fell ill, then they had black spots of dead flesh covering their body and died a painful but quick death.

Tepes, whose family saw many people a day, soon felt the pain that the plaque had to bring. Bolek soon started to feel ill. Worried for his family's safety, he quarantined himself in an old shed, hoping to ride out the sickness there.

Within a day, Bolek started to see black circles on his body and knew that he was about to die. Two days later, he was gone. Scared of the sickness, there was no funeral, even though the hurt was a bit too much. The family wailed in ache and agony. The town burnt down the old shed, hoping to rid the town of both his sick body and the sickness itself. Unfortunately, it was too late: the sickness was now in Bram.

Distort over losing his young son, Tepes headed out into the country for a few days while his wife and kids mourned their loss. The town was still in demand of his work, so he had to return.

Over the next few weeks, no one else got sick, and everyone believed the troubling times to be over. Just then, without warning, the school principal started coughing up blood. He broke out in those black death spots and began to tell the people that he loved them, wishing them goodbyes. Right after that, he fell to the floor, lifeless, dead. Unknowing, he had spread the sickness to more people, worsening the problem. The disease started to spread very fast and killed even faster.

Within a month, a third of the town was dead or was dying. The deceased were burnt, and the sick were kept locked in their homes until they died. No one could survive once they had become ill. The town was paralyzed with fear. As the problem grew, stores, churches, schools, and almost everything were closed as people hid in fear.

Tepes, Raina, Zora, and Peti were all spared from the sickness so far and were able to help those who were sick without becoming sick themselves. Raina believed it was because they followed the word of God and that they had God's protection from the sickness: so it was their job to tend to the sick and help them the best they could. So, even against the will and Tepe's better judgment, they reopened the shop and started to give aid to all the sick and dying people of Bram.

But, in time, even with all the best of intentions, this would prove to be a fatal mistake that would change the Tupaco family and the town of Bram forever.

Chapter 5

As the town tried to survive the madness that had taken over, the townsfolk could only try and live as normal a life as possible. In the meanwhile, only a selected few were willing to be as brave as to take the risk of trying to help the people who were not so lucky. There were many who were sick, and only a few came forward to help. Only a few amongst them were courageous enough to help. The people in town were terrified of what may happen to each of them as the sickness spread across their small beloved town.

Raina and the two daughters were the town's shining light. Even after the loss of a son, a brother, and a cherished and loved family member, they continued to brave the storm and face the great sickness. They stepped forward in taking food to the sick and to the well. They would bring water, and when it would be time, they would cremate the bodies.

Very few only were willing to take the risk and go into the town's sick areas to help. Tepes was scared of losing his family, and he disapproved. Still, he could not help but respect the women of his family for their bravery and their selflessness. He knew that without their hard work, more people would suffer. He knew that if it weren't for these three, there would be more and more bodies piling up. It needed to be done.

He continued to fix shoes for those who were still willing to travel. With work slowing down, he did not need his family's help to run the shop, but as he worked, he still worried about the grave danger that his wife and daughters were facing unflinchingly.

With the passage of time, the sick and dying became less and less, and the people started to see the light at the end of the tunnel. They thought that the black death was about to run its course, and the town and life may be able to get back to normal. Yet they knew not that there was a lot more to come, a ton of terror that was waiting for them just around the corner.

As Tepes' family thrived while helping the needs of the people, Tepes could feel a slow change in himself, not one he was hoping to ever see. As he worked, he slowly started to feel tired more and more with the passage of each day and the arrival of each moon. Even with a lighter workload and extra rest, he just could not get his energy levels back to normal.

After a week of feeling helpless and sad, he began to have a small cough. Little did he know that it was the first sign of his impending doom. He had hid it well from Raina. Tepes knew that he could not hide it forever. While working, the worst had started to happen. As he would cough, he would start to spit up blood. Tepes now worried for the future of his family, knowing that no one in town had lived after this would happen to them. He knew his fate. This was his death sentence.

While he kept working in the shop and his family helping those in need, he was able to keep it from them for a week. Though hard it was, indeed.

It was a Friday afternoon when Tepes met his family for dinner. It was then that his wife and kids saw black circles over his face and arms. They panicked and started to cry, knowing that it was only a matter of time before he would pass.

Tepes told them that he had planned for the worse and would make sure that his family would be taken care of after he was gone. Being a strong fighter, Tepes held on for almost two weeks as his darling wife and beautiful daughters tended to his every need. But deep down, they were all quite desolate as they watched the head of their family being slowly taken from them. This was, indeed, a sad chapter in the histories of the family and the town itself.

In his small home, surrounded by his wife and daughters, Tepes joined his son in death. Tepes was now at peace. Raina, being with Tepes since they were in their mid-teens, could not burn her husband's body. She loved him too much and could not handle the idea that he was really gone. And for the first time in a long time, Bram had a real funeral at the very same graveyard that he once took care of.

He had a large funeral, and that was because the whole town knew him and respected him as a pillar of the village. In a sad event, everyone who lived in the town and knew Tepes came to pay their respects, and with that, life went on in Bram. Tepes' story was over.

But for how long?

Chapter 6

The town mourned the loss of such an important member of the community for the weeks to come. After he had gone, dead at 45 years of age, there was a large hole left in the community, an abyss never to be filled. His friends, his family, and the people he helped sat around and told stories about him every day, and they were learning to cope with their loss as time went on.

Once again, strange people start to pass through Bram with outrageous stories, stories of vampires. One tired traveler stayed the night as he was crossing the country and told the people of Bram that he had to leave his hometown because he was fleeing a monster, a vampire.

As they sat at a fire in the middle of the town, a new visitor began to tell the tales of the vampire. The townspeople who were in a small mountain community still believed that this was just a campfire story. They could just not believe any word of it, but they still listened to the story and learned the tale of this new and scary creature. They were curious to know, some of them afraid, some of them giggling at the preposterous and comical things the storyteller had to say.

As the story started, he told the people that this was not a work of fiction but the truth behind the evilest thing the devil had ever set loose on God's green earth. He said to them that a vampire is born when a person dies too soon due to sickness or murder.

"A vampire is born in a shallow grave," he said to them, the fire from the woods burning before him to give off a reflection of the fire over his face, "and so, everyone who is buried should be buried deep in the ground and lay face down to keep them from coming back and escaping. This creature always hunts at night, not because sunlight harms him, although it will speed up the rotting process of the corps, so it can find its victims when their sleeping. This is very much a zombie-like creature that must drink blood to stay alive. It must drain a body dead to keep itself alive for half a day, and it weakens the longer it goes without the blood. The creature hides at night and never makes a sound because it has no effect on animals. It does not recognize its presence as guard dogs do nothing to protect you. They enter your home at night and bite."

The people seemed disturbed by what he was saying, but they chose to listen. They were curious. "First, they aim for your heart, but they bite your neck if you move. As it feeds on you and blood returns to its body, its black eyes fill with blood and begin to look like brimstone. The creature will only feed on people it knew when it was alive and will not attack strangers or new people it may come across. It will just avoid them. It never kills at. First, it stalks its food. It always stalks its victims for three nights before it feeds. The first night it enters the home and identifies the target. On the second night, it goes back and marks the prey with a small scratch on its forehead. It is on the third night that the vampire will come in and go for the kill and drain its victim of all its blood."

A few of the gentlemen also sitting by the fire laughed. The man continued, however, to tell the tale, a warning he was giving to the people for their own safety, "They do not have fangs like an animal. They just bite into the body with whatever teeth it still had at the time of death. If you find a vampire's grace, the soil around it will not be disturbed as he will leave his grave, leaving no trace of movement. The only thing that can scare a vampire is a cross made of pig bones. Bibles, holy water, garlic, sunlight, and the church will do nothing to fend off this monster. The only way to kill a vampire is to kill its heart with a silver steak. Even if you can decapitate one, you still have to kill the heart." The people around the fire found the story both scary and disturbing but still said it was just a story.

Over the next few days, the story started to spread across Bram and started to have a few of the locals worried. Little had they known that their worry was justified. Little did they know that the ones who were laughing would soon be crying, worried, desperate, aching.

As people lived their lives and overlooked the graveyard, something terrible was about to take place there. Tepes' grave was a shallow one due to it being dug by a couple of very small ladies, and the ground was very hard. On top of that, he had died young due to disease, just as the visitor had warned about a vampire's genesis.

A change was taking place.

This once-treasured and still beloved member of Bram was experiencing a change that would be horrific. As he lay in his grave, his hair and nails continued to grow, and his body did not decompose like a normal corpse should.

Then one night, weeks after his funeral, he aroused. Tepes now inherited the vampire's curse, and with him knowing everyone who lived in Bram, no one was safe. As he arose, he was no longer a man but more of a mindless monster.

Within a week, two had already died by his hand. The people did not know what to think other than they had a killer in their town.

They could not find any suspects as the weeks went on, but the nighttime murders kept on coming. Rumors that just maybe a vampire really had come to Bram as this idea grew, so did the people's fears. As the people remember the stories they were told of the vampire, they are confused because it only killed people it knew in life. Yet people all over town in different groups were dying. They had made it their custom to burn bodies, not to bury the dead.

Then it hit Raina. It could only be Tepes. He knew everyone in town and was the only person who was buried after several years of people being burnt. Heartbroken, she knew the truth, and the legend of Tepes, the vampire, was born. The family went to Tepes' grave and dug it up, and their fear came true. The grave was empty.

Chapter 7

In a safe house in Paris, France, lies a wounded hunter. A monster hunter, he is healing from a lost battle he endured a few months ago in Egypt. He had single-handedly fought a group of vampires, but this time, he had lost.

Now an older man approaching his 60th birthday, he has dedicated his whole life to fighting monsters. Ever since he was a child, he had never been the one to be afraid or shy away from the monsters that kept others awake at night. He has battled creatures that most people believed to be not real, monsters that people could not even think about. He has fought and killed creatures that made other people shiver at the mere thought of them.

He has killed hags, werewolves, river monsters, cryptates, and vampires. He was orphaned as a child by a vampire and was saved by a great African holy man and hunter. He was the one who raised him as his own and taught him how to kill evil. He had always been derived from revenge, a spirit of vengeance that would never give up.

In Egypt, he was in a great battle that almost killed him. In a rare loss, he had to retreat and flee to Europe to find shelter and heal from his wounds. That was what led him to Paris. Here, he has spent months trying to recover from the injuries he suffered from the fight. This man's name is Akachi Anaya. His name, Akachi, means "God's hand;" Anaya means "an admirer of God."

He is an African man, a holy man, a monster hunter. He is from Ghana; this tall and slender man knows how to hunt and kill every type of evil that walks the earth. His hunts have led him to battle in Africa, Europe, and Asia. He is the only hunter left to stop these creatures. Afraid that if he ever stood still, the creatures he has ever hunted would find him. So, he has never had a home; all he owns is what he carries with him each place he goes – black boots, a black hat, black pants, and a black coat. He carries a small bag of tools that he uses to hunt the monsters. His most prized possession is his Bible. It's not, however, a normal Bible; it's the Vampire Bible.

It is a 1000-page book written in blood. It has the history of the vampire in it, along with everything that is known about the creatures. It further talks about all the possible ways to kill all the possible creatures. What makes this book special is that the Bible is wrapped in a very special cover; the cover is made from the very tablecloth used by Jesus at the last supper. It was the same tablecloth used to feed his disciples. It is believed that this helps protect the book and its holder; it was given to Akachi by his mentor and father figure Semi. This is his most important tool.

Akachi believes that he was chosen by God to eliminate evil and has given his life to that notion. As Akachi reflects on what happened in his last battle and what went wrong, he hears about the travelers' rumors about a new terror. As he lies there, he asks a visitor to tell him the story that they were just telling the others. He assured Akachi that this was the truth, and he began with the story that many others believed to be tales and folklores.

He told him of a new evil in Romania in a small town that no one ever even knew about. Akachi asks what the name of this town is, and the guy says to him, "The town is called Bram. It is in Romania in the forest somewhere."

In Bram, the great sickness has killed a lot of people. Though it had passed, it created a new sickness, a sickness called Tepes or, as the locals called him, The Night Stalker. He tells Akachi of all the deaths that have been occurring there through the nights and all the victims having their hearts bitten out of their bodies. Akachi was told that the grave of a man named Tepes Tupaco was found empty.

Akachi now sees his next target and asks for a map of Europe. He is weeks away from making it to Romania and must cross the dangerous and rough Carpathians Mountain range. From France, there is only one way to get into Romania – the Borgo Pass. Luckily for Akachi, it will lead him straight into the village of Bram. As he feels that he has healed enough to travel and believes he will be healed by the time he reaches the pass, he decides that the hunt for Tepes, The Night Stalker is on.

With the moral and warm people around him giving him what he needs to make the long trip, he heads out alone to find his prey. Braving a snowstorm in the mountains, he finds the Borgo Pass and marches into Bram with confidence that no one had ever seen before. There, he hopes to find Tepes, hoping to get into a one-on-one battle with him and put an end to these killings in Bram.

Romania is a new land for Akachi, and he is unsure of how the local people will react to his presence when he introduces himself. As the snow starts to fall, too slow, he reaches the town. He is the only hope the village has, and they welcome him with open arms, hoping and praying that he can end the curse of the vampire that had been cast upon their small town. With the support of the people and a lifetime of experience behind him, he hopes that he can finally stop the terror of The Night Stalker once and for all, expectantly before he gets the chance to take the whole town.

Chapter 8

In Bram, fear begins to grow. Each week more townspeople of Bram are found missing and then dead. They are always found outside of town, impaled on a large wooden pole. Their bodies are almost totally drained of blood and suspended high in the air.

This is terrifying for the people of Bram as they watch their friends and family gets taken from them, and so far, there is nothing that they can do to stop from being the next victim of Tepes.

They have tried having a night watch team Rome the streets after dark, they lock their doors and windows, and nothing seems to protect them, and the police and the night watch team can't find their deadly killer. Every week more and more people fall victim and end up hanging on a pole with their life force removed. For those chosen by the beast, they have no knowledge that it was in their home watching them sleep the night before, and when they wake up, they will find a strange mark on their forehead, and their fear comes true because after your marked, you die, and as of now no one has been able to be protected from Tepes.

With rumors going around about a new strange visitor that has come to town, the people are desperate to know if it's true, has a savior has come to rid their town of this darkness. Knowing about the rumors of his arrival in Bram Akachi keeps them in suspense as he keeps his whereabouts unknown as he plans his attack to stop his new foe. After weeks of trying to get a plan of attack, he can't find much information on Tepes and decides it's time to officially make his presence known. In the middle of town, he calls everyone to meet him in the town square. Excited to find out that the rumors of a powerful hunter are true, the whole town shows up in hopes of finding a way to stop the killings. Here he makes his introduction and tells the town that he was in Bram to rid them of Tepes.

During this very long speech, Akachi educates the people on what it is that is killing them, how to protect themselves, and how he has beaten this creature before. He asks the townspeople to put a cross made of pig's bones over their doors and windows. It's one of the few things that may work. He tells them that the police and the night watch team will not stop the impaling. Just stay inside and out of his way. As Akachi starts to hunt his prey, he finds this beast to be much more intelligent and cunning than most he has slain. Whether it was skill, luck, or instinct, Tepes was very hard to find and was great at avoiding attention, even slipping into guarded homes and pulling out the bodies undetected. Nevertheless, Akachi loved a challenge and would continue the hunt.

It was now time for Akachi to put all his skill, tricks, and experience to work to take down this undead being. With a never-ending blood bath, Bram was now a killing field. Everyone in Bram was now looking at their new dark hunter for hope, and Akachi was not about to disappoint. Akachi knew it would only be a matter of time before he would find Tepes and that he was safe from being attacked for now. Tepes never knew Akachi in life; therefore, he would not be a target. However, to get his battle with the vampire, he would need to trap, catch, or attack it in order to do battle. Only then could he end the terror of Tepes' killing spree by ripping his heart out of his body and destroying it. Only then would Tepes be stopped.

With the village putting all their faith on Akachi's shoulders, Akachi gets hard to work. First, he starts looking at what homes were chosen and in what order they were attacked and mapping where the impaling was at, and starts looking for a pattern. Akachi also wondered why Tepes had not yet attacked his family. He did know them the best out of everyone in town and should be a prime target for this nasty monster. As he maps Tepes' attacks, he sees a pattern.

The impaled bodies were found all in a line. The first bodies were found near Tepes' grave and were wrapping north around town, creating a circle around Bram. Even more, telling was that the Tupaco family lived close to the center of town. The attacks started at the homes on the outside of town and were spiraling in a circle through town, slowly working their way to the middle of town. Akachi now knows what is happening.

Tepes is saving his wife and kids for last. He was killing the townspeople in a circle pattern, and when he was done, he would take his family's life last. This could be to give his family a little bit more time to live, it could be that he sees them as a trophy, or it could just be that this creature is just working his way across town trying to stay alive, and they just happen to live in the last home attacked. Learning of this pattern, Akachi starts to watch the homes he thinks will be hit next. Unfortunately, Tepes is not as mindless as most vampires.

Now, he is no longer the man he once was but now a spawn of Satan. He knew he was being hunted and was able to avoid being found. But, as Akachi thought, the deaths kept coming in a spiral pattern, and the impalements that started at Tepes' grave still appeared outside of town. Being unable to grab the beast in the act, Akachi studies the attacks and starts to pull people out of their homes at night and into a safe house so that when Tepes makes his way into a home, he will find it empty.

After only a week of doing this, the killings seemed to stop, the plan had worked, and Tepes had not been able to find his next victim to feed on. The people hoped that this would weaken the vampire by starving him and making it easier to kill him. Unfortunately, this only angered the monster, and after going hungry for a week, he started his stalking in the early and late part of the day and still was able to mark his prey.

Even if people felt safe during the day, Tepes started feeding on them before the sun went down, and the impaled bodies were found outside of town the next morning, and now half the town had fallen to the terror of this hungry vampire.

Chapter 9

Akachi being a man of great faith, kneeled and prayed for help in stopping this killer. Akachi knew that with the help of God and his old friend Semi watching over him, he would find a way to stop Tepes. As he was silent in prayer in the town's holy church, he felt the spirit of his old mentor Semi arrives. As he is in prayer, he seeks Semi's wisdom and advice.

He could not talk directly to Semi but felt his warm presence and knew it was a sign that he would prevail in his quest. With his confidence renewed, he stands to his feet and thanks God for sending an angel to watch over him and leaves this holy place. Akachi's mind starts to think of every battle he has ever had with a vampire. He thought about what their strengths were.

They were very elusive, strong, great hunters, and hard to kill. But what were their weaknesses? They can't swim, are normally alone, only as fast as an average man, and even after death, they are still mortal and able to die. His only goal was to save the people of Bram by freeing Tepes from his curse so his soul could travel to heaven and take another slave away from the devil. For in Akachi eyes, Tepes was a victim of this curse and had no control over it, and therefore was not guilty of what he had done.

Still, it was the devil himself to blame and to set Tepes free. He must end his curse by destroying his heart and take a stab at Satan himself by taking away one of his enslaved souls. Akachi must stop Tepes from taking any more lives away from God and rid Bram of this nightmare. The more Akachi watches the town, the more he learns. he is now moving people from one place to another, and now no one goes anywhere in groups of less than three in the daylight hours. It was working. No one had been killed in many days. Tepes still only find empty homes and can't attack during daylight due to the number of people that are always around.

The effort is paying off, but Akachi knows that it won't last forever and that the only answer is to find and stop the vampire so the people of Bram can live their lives in peace. Tepes can't go without fresh blood forever, and Akachi knows that he will soon start to weaken and will become desperate to find a victim, and doing so will put him in a very dangerous position. As he tries to feed on the town, there is not a single victim to be found, and for Akachi, this will give him the opportunity to put an end to this killing machine. As the days go by and Tepes can't find a victim, the people of Bram grow in faith that their newfound friend Akachi is getting closer to stopping Tepes.

For more than two weeks now, there have been no marks, no murders, and no impaling outside of town. Akachi wonders what Tepes is waiting for. He must be starving at this point. Akachi starts to form a plan, a plan that the people of Bram may not like. Akachi wants to use live humans as bait to draw Tepes in. He wants to use the Tupaco family as bait to catch the beast but to do this, he would be putting the Tupaco family at great risk. If the trap does not work, at least one member of the family will lose their life. As he puts it together, he hates the thought of bringing it in front of the townspeople, for they may hate him for it, but he must make them see that it is the only way to bring peace and happiness to Bram and stop Tepes, it's a risk, but they must take it.

In the middle of the day, a time he knows Tepes would not be hunting, he calls a meeting, and as the family of Tepes is by his side and with a deep and worrying breath, he begins to tell the people his plan and what he wants to do. He tells the people that the home in the center of town is where they will set the trap. He wants to dig a large and deep pit around the home filled with water and large spiked poles to trap Tepes. This would have to be dug, spikes placed, filled halfway with water, and covered with limbs, straw, and soil so as to look normal and not be spotted by Tepes in only one day, a large task for anyone.

At this point, the people were all in on this idea, but then in front of everyone, Akachi asked Raina and her children to stay in the home and be the bait for their former loved one. He told them that there was a great risk to their lives by doing this, but if they could trap Tepes in the pit, he could kill him. The people of Bram respected the great hunter, but all started to shout and yell that the risk was too great and that there had to be a better way. Raina stood up in front of everyone and said that there was no other way, and this terror had to stop. She alone would stay the night in the house as bait and wait for what was once her husband to come for her. In shock, the crowd fell silent.

Her children said they would stay and help her, but Raina said no, it had to be her, and she would draw him in. Akachi and Raina walk toward each other and shake hands, both knowing this could kill Raina if anything goes wrong. The only issue is they must dig the trap wide and deep in only a few hours on that day and need enough spikes to trap a monster. This will take every man, woman, and child in Bram to pull off.

Akachi gives Raina, her children, and the townspeople a few days to physically and mentally prepare for what must be done. Then, as the people settle in for nightfall and hide from

Tepes, Akachi returns to the church to pray for the safety of Raina and hopes he is making the right decision. After an hour of prayer, he feels a hand on his shoulder, and as he looks to see who it is beside him, he sees a faint figure, almost ghost-like, standing with him. His friend Semi has come one last time to assure Akachi that what he is doing is correct and that God is pleased with his service to him. Then just like fog Semi disappears. Akachi must now rest, for he has work to do and knows his final showdown with this great predator will soon be at hand.

Rest now, Akachi. Your battle draws near.

Chapter 10

With the plan set, Raina knows her days are few with her family and spends all the time she can with them and mentally prepares to face what is left of her husband, knowing she must help him rest in peace. With her children, they settle in for the night, say a prayer, and head to bed. Her children can hardly sleep, knowing the danger that their mother will soon be in. As Akachi sleeps, he has a very vivid dream.

He feels like he is in a cloud and in his mind has already battled Tepes; bad sleep is better than no sleep for the dark hunter, but he sees it as a sign that he is ready to defeat his dark, evil enemy. As Tepes contuse to stalk the town at night, his hunger grows. It's been quite a while since his last meal, and his thirst and hunger are becoming unbearable and almost out of control. Without fresh blood and only finding empty homes, he feels his body growing weak and starting to rot. The smell alone could give his presence away, and he must find a meal soon. The time to prepare their mind and soul is over, and the day has come to build the trap, and every able-bodied person in town has shown up to make sure the trap is set and end the terror of Tepes. As promised, Akachi is ready.

He takes total control of the townspeople and puts them to work. The larger, stronger men of Bram start to dig the pit. It's very large, twenty feet across and ten feet deep, and circles the entire house. This is a huge task that must be done in hours. The rest of the men set out to find the wood they needed to make lots of spiked poles for the pit, along with branches to lay across the top to make a weak roof. The women and children gather straw and leave to try and cover the gaps in it so that when they are done, they can cover it with sand and hide the death trap.

With everyone working hard, they get it done working from mid-morning to midafternoon to avoid Tepes. Akachi is pleased that they had the trap set and even pulled enough water from a nearby stream to fill the pit with water four feet deep, a proud day for all involved.

With the night drawing closer, the town returns to their hiding places and will have to wait till the morning to see if Tepes has been killed. To prepare for battle, Akachi wears his cross of pig bones, has a blade made of bronze and silver ready, puts his precious Bible in his breast pocket, and begins to meditate to clear his mind and wait for Raina's signal to attack. Raina, who appears very calm, sits in the small house with a light burning to let Tepes know the home is not empty. She goes into her nightly routine of getting ready for bed. With the light burning and pig bones over the windows, they know that if this vampire gets past the trap, he will come in through the front door.

In the mountain woods just outside of town, a hungry vampire makes his way into town to quench his thirst and end his hunger. Tepes, who is starving, start going house to house looking for a meal until he sees the light in the windows, and as he gets so close, he can smell a familiar smell, his wife, his best friend, his food, Raina. Without making a sound, he heads straight towards the house. As he approaches, he does not realize that Akachi is just outside the pit, waiting to attack.

As Tepes reaches the house, he stops. It's dark, and Tepes can see only slightly better than a person in the dark. He knows something is not right.

As he steps onto the top of the pit, he can feel it give and stops. Being a crafty creature, he slides down into the pit, crosses it, and climbs out the other side without being noticed. Tepes climbs to the top of the pit and glares at the home. He peeks into the window to see Rania lying on the bed with her back to him. Tepes starts looking for a way into the home, finds the door unlocked, enters the home, and makes no noise. Unaware of his arrival Raina lies in her bed, waiting for her encounter with him. Tepes is almost amazed to see her again and just stands in the doorway and stares at her. Deep inside, somewhere, he almost remembers his love for her, but the man who had that love is dead.

Raina rolls over to see him standing there. Too scared to scream, she just looks at what has happened to her husband. His hair had fallen out, eyes sank into his head, skin rotting, and no signs of the once-intelligent human being in him at all. Tepes starts to move towards Raina; his hunger takes over, and he attacks. Raina lets out a loud scream and makes a run at the front door, but as she opens the door, Tepes grabs her and goes for the bite. Raina hits him as hard as she can and breaks free as Tepes misses his bite.

Now Raina fears her biggest problem; she can't run because of the pit, but she stands her ground with hopes of finding her lost husband somewhere inside him. Unfortunately, the man she loved was no longer there. Just as she fears that Tepes is going to take her, Akachi runs across a makeshift bridge across the pit and tackles Tepes. Raina is terrified beyond belief and runs across the rickety bridge to escape back into town, but she can't help but stop and watch the battle.

After the tackle, they both roll across the ground, and as the vampire tries to stand, the edge of the pit gives way, and he falls into the pitch-black dark pit. Without hesitation, Akachi follows him down into the dark death trap. It's dark, everything is pitch black, and the hunter can see nothing, hearing the monster moving around in the water, Akachi tries to focus on where Tepes is at.

The townspeople heard the noise, and all ran out to their trap to help their hunter. They put their torches down inside the pit and know Akachi can see everything inside the pit. Tepes, hungry and feeling no fear, only a thirst for blood, tries to bite Akachi, but he dodges the attack and lays his cross of pig bones on top of Tepes' head, which enraged the beast more. Tepes breaks a spike in half and starts to attack Akachi with it, but Akachi defends. Akachi and Tepes have a knockdown bare-knuckle brawl inside the fire-lit pit, and Tepes starts to gain the advantage over this mighty hunter and picks Akachi up over his head and charges at a large spike in the pit. He's going to end the life of this great holy warrior.

Not going down without a fight, Akachi manages to spin out of Tepes' grip, and using his own momentum, he impales Tepes onto the spike just as Tepes had done to so many people in Bram. Missing his heart Tepes moans as he tries to pull himself off the steak, but Akachi pins him down using another steak. Finally, Akachi reads Tepes his last rights, and using his silver-covered knife, he cuts out the heart of Tepes and impales it on another pole. With the curse broken, Tepes' soul is set free, and the killer vampire is vanquished.

Exhausted from the fight, the people of Bram help Akachi climb out of the pit and celebrate the victory. The next day a huge celebration is planned to honor the hunter's work, but Akachi is not to be seen. His work in Bram is finished, and now he must return to Africa and end the monster that injured him and killed his mentor Semi.

Finally, the smoke had cleared. The danger was gone. The town was safe again.